Best Wishes!

Werner Zimmermann

# ZERO
# IS NOT ENOUGH

### H. Werner Zimmermann

TORONTO  OXFORD  NEW YORK
OXFORD UNIVERSITY PRESS
1990

Ahhh! It's Hallowe'en, the time for trick or treaters.

It's a good thing we've got lots and lots of candies.

Don't they look delicious?

We'd better be sure we have enough.
Maybe we should count them.

You write the numbers
while I count the candies.

**One.**
If I were the tooth fairy,
it would be sweet
to have just one.

**Two.**
And if I were a pirate,
I'd be sure to take two.

**Three.**
But if I were a witch,
I could put a spell on three.

**Four.**
No, wait! If I were a ghost,
I would moan and groan for four.

**Five.**
But if I were a giant,
I could **FEE, FI, FO** five!

**Six.**
Hold on. If I were a wizard,
I'd make six disappear.

**Seven.**
And if I were a vampire,
I'd slurp seven juicy, red ones.

**Eight.**
Better yet! If I were a mummy,
I'd eat eight—
still in their wrappers.

# Nine.
Aha! If I were King Kong,
I'd dine on nine.

**Ten.**
Oh, wait. Wait! If I were a hairy,
scary monster,

# Zero.
Do you mean we have nothing left?